DEATH BY SPREADSHEET

A Detective Story of Governance, Grit, and the SAP 'Migrate Your Data' App

Isard Haasakker

No Tie Generation Limited

a SAP SOAP Story

ISBN-13 (E-book): 978-1-9193089-0-6
ISBN-13 (Paperback): 978-1-9193089-1-3

www.SAPsoap.com
www.NoTieGeneration.com

For my wife.

CONTENTS

FOREWORD

This story grew out of thirty years inside real SAP projects, the kind that stretch patience, sleep, and logic in equal measure.

Every scene has a heartbeat I have heard somewhere before. The names, companies, and timelines have been changed, sometimes merged, sometimes disguised, but the emotions are untouched.

I did not set out to write a manual. I wanted to capture the human side of transformation: how people behave when deadlines breathe down their necks and data refuses to behave. If it feels familiar, that is because it probably is.

I'll step aside now. The next voice you'll hear belongs to Alex, and the chaos she's about to walk into.

Isard

PROLOGUE

If you're reading this, you've probably survived at least one project that felt like a hostage situation with spreadsheets. Congratulations. You made it out alive. Mostly.

Before we start, a confession. I used to think structure would save me. That a perfectly formatted status report could stop chaos. Spoiler: it can't. You can colour-code a crisis all you want; it's still on fire.

My story isn't a manual. It's a collection of scars pretending to be lessons. The pattern is predictable: optimism, denial, panic, Excel. Then caffeine, sarcasm, and a faint hope that someone knows what they're doing. Usually they don't. Sometimes that someone is me.

If you've ever nodded in a meeting while thinking "what on earth are we doing?", we're practically siblings. I've been there, eyes twitching at PowerPoint animations, watching confidence decay faster than a test environment on a Friday night. You're safe here. This is a judgement-free zone. Well, mostly. I still judge poor documentation.

I'll keep the jargon light and the honesty heavy. The goal isn't to make you smarter; it's to make you feel slightly less mad for caring about a system that clearly doesn't. Think of me as that colleague who blurts out the truth mid-meeting, usually at the wrong time and after too much coffee.

Now, about SOAP.

You probably expect me to talk about: Simple Object Access Protocol. It was built so machines could talk politely while humans shouted across meeting rooms. "Let the systems handle it," they said. "They don't get emotional." Except they do. Ever seen a server throw a tantrum on a Friday? That's emotion.

My SOAP is different. It's not about systems. It's about the humans behind them: Structured. Open. Aligned. Purified.

Four words that sound like a mindfulness app but are really survival tactics.

Structured, because chaos spreads exponentially. Open, because silence is lethal. Aligned, because pretending to agree is the slowest form of sabotage. Purified, because sooner or later everything needs a good scrub. That includes data, process, and your ego.

I'm not promising miracles, just proof that things fall apart and still function afterwards. Like most of us.

Now grab a drink, silence your notifications, and follow me into the boardroom.

It's Tuesday, the coffee's burnt, and the honeymoon period is already over.

Alex

1. A DAGGER IN THE MIND

Some rooms are built for triumph. This one prefers autopsies.

The boardroom gleams with the false confidence of glass and chrome, polished to hide the bruises underneath. The flagship sapwood soap bars line one wall, sealed in acrylic boxes, proof that Sapura Cosmetics still worships the sap-sweet scent that started it all. A table big enough for peace talks stretches beneath a row of immaculate lights, every surface reflecting someone's need for control. The projector hums at the far end, casting numbers that flicker like nervous lies. The air tastes of polished wood and panic. Where new money meets stale ambition.

Tuesday morning. Week two of acceptance testing. The honeymoon period is over. The hangover has begun. The enthusiasm that fills the kick-off slides curdles into a quiet, nervous silence. You can almost hear the collective thought: *please don't let it be my fault.*

Alex sits near the head of the table, back straight, notebook open, pen balanced like a weapon she hopes not to use. The white light from the projector washes her skin to paper, throwing small shadows beneath her eyes, evidence of too many nights chasing other people's mistakes. She pulls her hair back just enough to suggest effort, not approval. Calm posture, tired eyes, clear intent: the holy trinity for any project manager.

Across the room, the usual suspects whisper like students before an exam. Fluorescent light hums, pretending to be order in a room full of chaos. Alex studies the symmetry of misery and thinks, if silence had Key Performance Indicators, they'd all exceed target.

The chair at the end stays empty, framed in pale light, the kind reserved for villains who appear only when the damage is measurable.

Opposite Alex sits Claire, recently promoted for reasons still under corporate investigation. Her blonde hair is coiled into a bun so exact it could pass a compliance audit. A silk scarf - pale blue, tied with the precision of someone who alphabetises emotions - rests at her throat. Light glances off her pearl earrings, catching the faint movement of a jaw that's been clenched through too many meetings. Every gesture is measured, polished, and faintly exhausting, as if perfection itself were part of her job description.

When she finally speaks, her voice slices through the murmur. "We're seeing several issues from the business users." She pauses for effect, scanning faces like rows of data. "Missing fields. Wrong units. Duplicates."

Alex freezes. The words fall like bombs. Claire's tone stays calm, but the pause that follows is deliberate, engineered for maximum discomfort. Then, slowly, inevitably, that gaze turns to Alex.

"They say it's slowing them down. They can't complete testing."

Alex feels twenty heads rotate towards her. The room shrinks by half. She clears her throat, ready to respond, but Claire lifts a finger, gentle, almost kind. "I've already escalated it."

A ripple of unease moves through the room. Someone shifts a chair. A pen clicks.

The door opens. The room holds its breath.

Richard steps in, Sapura's CEO and final authority, the kind of man whose silence travels faster than his words. His shaved head catches the light like polished steel, his suit immaculate, his expression carved from calm. He doesn't stride; he glides. A man so practised at control that even gravity seems to defer to him. The air tightens as he takes his seat at the head of the table, one slow, deliberate motion that says the review has already begun.

"I've been briefed," he says. His tone has that calm weight people mistake for fairness.

The room doesn't move. It just *waits.*

"The disruption during acceptance testing is unacceptable. We're behind schedule. We cannot afford delays."

He doesn't raise his voice, but the silence that follows is total. Alex's pen hovers above her notebook.

Then the blade lands. "Alex, I want you to find the root cause and give me a resolution plan. One week."

One week. The corporate unit of impossible.

A few people exhale in relief; others stare into their papers as though studying grief. Alex feels her jaw tighten. "Understood," she says, steady but flat.

The meeting continues, words buzzing around her like wasps. Alex writes furiously, though half the notes are nonsense, doodles disguising panic. Claire keeps speaking, her tone smooth as glass. It's an Oscar-worthy performance. Alex knows it, but she can't stop wondering: is this premeditated, or did Claire see an opportunity and take it?

When the meeting finally collapses under its own weight, chairs scrape and laptops snap shut. People flee in polite haste, leaving the room echoing and too bright. Alex stays behind, staring at her notes as if they magically rearrange into answers.

She waits until the door clicks closed, then releases the breath she's been holding.

The coffee machine in the corner blinks like a tiny robot begging to help. She presses the button; it growls in protest before coughing out a cup of something resembling courage. The air smells of burnt beans and lost ideas. She takes a sip and winces. Hope was never meant to taste this bitter.

She leans against the counter, staring at the now-empty table. Moments ago, it was a battlefield. Now it looks innocent again, polished and waiting for the next execution.

She steps to the window and presses her palm to the glass. The city still runs below her, bright veins of light ignoring her absence. Her reflection looks back: pale, sharp, blazer creased, hair escaping in small acts of defiance. Good. She's done playing immaculate. She studies the woman in the glass the way she studies systems: looking for the failure point. Her reflection blinks once, slow, as if tired of pretending. The eyes looking back are tired but alert. *Still here,* they say. *Still fixing things no one sees.*

Fine. Let them throw deadlines. She's survived worse.

Her mind starts piecing it together. Missing fields. Duplicate data. Testing delays. All of it points somewhere, but where? She flips open her notebook. Every note feels like a clue to a mystery wrapped in secrets. A detective without a badge, she tells herself. Or perhaps the usual project manager, cleaning up crimes disguised as 'lessons learned.'

She imagines the SAP users describing the issues. "It's not working. It used to work in the old system." Translation: chaos without clarity. Somewhere, someone has turned a simple migration into modern art.

The more she thinks, the more the sarcasm steadies her pulse. "Of course it's fine," she mutters. "It's just the data equivalent of a house built on sand."

She sips again. The taste of lukewarm determination.

The reflection in the window catches her eye once more. "Right," she says to the window. "Let's find out who broke what."

The fluorescent light flickers overhead, signalling its acceptance. She exhales, the tension easing just enough for a smile. "If they want clarity," she says quietly, "they'll get it. Unfiltered."

Captain's Log: Raiders Of The Lost Artefacts

R – Risks / Root Causes

- Data issues confirmed: missing fields, wrong units, duplicates.
- User testing blocked; migration logic collapsing.
- Structure exists only on slides - not in reality.

A – Actions

- Trace every failure back to source.
- Interview key business users, not just IT.
- Map the migration process end-to-end before touching fixes.
- Deliver a resolution plan in one week.

I – Impacts

- Acceptance testing stalled.
- Richard's patience measured in days, not weeks.
- Team morale dropping; silence replacing status.
- My credibility now tied to system behaviour.

D – Decisions / Dependencies

- Report directly to Richard.
- Ignore Claire's performance politics.
- Focus on facts, not fear.
- One week to prove structure still exists.

Current state: **Bewildered**

2. REBOOTING UNDER PRESSURE

Alex stands in her office and tries to carve calm from the chaos that follows her from the boardroom. The *SAP Activate* certificate glares from the wall, a framed reminder that awarded competence also has an expiry date. Half-closed blinds stripe the desk like a barcode, scanning the room. The air tastes thin with recycled tension.

She pulls the cord, flooding the room with light that feels far too cheerful for the kind of morning this is. The warmth hits her face, only tightening the knot in her stomach.

Binders line the shelf, spines dented from overuse, still pretending order exists. Her notebook lies open, revealing a battlefield of half-formed logic and coffee ghosts. She presses two fingers to her temple, as if she can reboot clarity manually.

Outside, footsteps hurry past, too quick, too loud. Through the blinds she spots Vanessa gliding by, clipboard in hand, expression set to *calm mode*. Her light-brown skin catches a stripe of morning sun, and a halo of tight curls softens her steady stride.

She is my project coordinator, keeps the daily machinery running. She bridges the gap between the business teams and IT, translating frustration into tasks, making sure updates, meetings, and documents flow to the right people. She's the person who knows who actually does what, and who forgot. One look from her says what no one else will: *we're in trouble, but breathe anyway*.

The sight of her steady stride tightens the pressure in Alex's chest.

She shuts the hallway blinds, turning her room into a makeshift prison, and sinks into her chair. The air-con whirs like a bored wasp. A half-empty bottle of water shivers slightly on the desk; even it seems nervous.

"Keep it together," she mutters. The words hang there, half pep talk, half threat. If you ever whisper that to yourself before a status meeting, you're in good company.

She breathes in, breathes out, and opens JIRA. The place where projects go to confess their sins. A to-do list with mood swings.

The dashboard blinks awake, as innocent as a crime scene before the detectives arrive. Tickets sprawl across the screen in no discernible logic: half thoughts, quarter details, heroic guesses. She scrolls. And frowns. Structure, clearly, is on annual leave.

Where's the disaster?

Claire describes a building on fire. JIRA offers a lukewarm shrug. A handful of minor issues, nothing worth panic pay. The mismatch crawls under her skin. If Claire is right, this system is hiding its sins, and Alex doesn't have the full picture. Control means nothing without truth.

She leans closer, scanning ticket after ticket. Each one feels rushed, as if someone filled it in during a fire drill. Descriptions taper off mid-sentence. Some tickets contain single words like *urgent* or *wrong*. Helpful. Others are blank except for a priority flag screaming *critical*, with no explanation why. It's chaos formatted as compliance.

Her irritation spikes. If silence is documentation, this project is flawless. She scrolls again, eyes narrowing. Claire's 'emergency' doesn't exist here. That means two things: the real issue isn't recorded, and Claire has information she hasn't shared. Both set Alex up for failure. Control, she knows, is the only thing standing between order and meltdown.

Her jaw clenches. 'Brilliant,' she mutters to herself. 'I'm supposed to fix a mystery built on missing evidence.'

The phone buzzes against the desk, nudging a pen to the floor. She catches it mid-roll, small victory. *Vanessa.* Of course.

"Morning, Alex," Vanessa says, voice calm but cautious, like someone approaching a wild animal with a clipboard. "I'm checking in. The team is nervous. They're hearing rumours about serious issues in the acceptance system."

"Rumours," Alex repeats. "Funny, I have a whole JIRA board and not a single ticket that looks like an emergency."

Vanessa sighs softly. "Claire briefed Richard this morning. He sounded... concerned."

"Concerned?" Alex can almost hear her heartbeat in the pause. "Based on what? I can't see half of what's supposedly burning down."

"I'm not sure," Vanessa admits. "But people are spooked. They're asking what to do."

Alex spins her chair towards the wall, forcing her tone steady. Sarcasm drips through anyway. "What to do? Easy. First, everyone stops panicking in whispers and starts writing in JIRA like grown adults. Second, they fill in the tickets properly. All of them. We can't solve what isn't documented."

Vanessa hesitates, then chuckles quietly. "Copy that. I'll rally them. But Alex... please take a breath. We need you steady, not defibrillating."

"Steady went out the window this morning," Alex says. The hint of humour in Vanessa's voice softens her mood. "Just keep them honest. Every missing detail is another day on this project's tombstone."

When the call ends, the silence feels heavier, but at least it's hers.

She drags a hand down her face and stares at the screen again. JIRA's glow paints her notebook blue, a digital confession of chaos. She needs structure. She needs facts. And she needs them fast.

Fine. If she can't trust the big picture, she'll start small.

She refreshes the board, and one ticket stands out like a sore thumb. **Wrong base unit of measure.** Normally, that would barely warrant a shrug. But this one has detail: multiple comments, screenshots, and even a few cross-references to other issues. Someone actually cares. A miracle.

Alex reads deeper. A pattern emerges. The ticket hints at faulty conversions, cascading errors, and mismatched stock units. It's the first thread she can pull. And threads, she knows, lead somewhere, if you're willing to bleed for the trail.

Her pulse steadies as she copies the ticket ID into her notes. Sam is the current owner.

Outside her cave, the office hums with routine oblivion: printers whir, keyboards clatter, phones trill. The soundtrack of denial.

She straightens, notebook in hand, and steps toward the corridor. "Alright," she murmurs. "Let's see what you're hiding."

Captain's Log: One Small Clue For Man, One Giant Raid For Mankind

R – Risks / Root Causes

- JIRA tickets incomplete; half the story missing.
- System sins hiding in plain sight.
- Claire sitting on key information.
- Setup engineered for my failure.
- Team jittery, powered by rumours not facts.

A – Actions

- Start small: one detailed ticket.
- Ticket ID traces a faulty base-unit conversion.
- Interview end-users who actually touch the data.
- Enforce proper JIRA entries - no blanks, no excuses.
- Build evidence trail before assumptions take over.

I – Impacts

- Claire's "emergency" still unverified.
- Executive concern fuelled by gossip, not logs.
- Compliance mask hiding chaos underneath.
- Panic is faster than proof.

D – Decisions / Dependencies

- Trust Vanessa's instincts; she reads the room better than reports.
- Tune out boardroom theatre.
- Focus on the technical root cause - one thread at a time.
- Follow the first ticket wherever it leads.

Current state: **Hunting for facts.**

3. WHAT YOU SEE IS NOT WHAT YOU GET

The room hums like an overworked server begging for early retirement. Three monitors blink like anxious eyes, their glow bleaching the colour from everything. The air smells of burnt coffee and overheated wires, like ambition cooked too long.

Sam sits in the centre, shoulders squared. Mid-forties, pale skin freckled from too many screens, red hair sticking up like static gone feral. His rolled sleeves reveal wiry forearms cross-hatched with the faint scratches of old hardware work, a body built on adrenaline and endurance. He's half-merged with his chair and the system he refuses to surrender to.

Sam is our data analyst and owns the technical logic behind how information moves from the old systems into SAP S/4HANA. He's the one who drills data until it confesses.

Alex observes Sam. This is what despair looks like in spreadsheet form. She steps in, heels clicking against the tiles, and the noise makes Sam flinch. He looks up, eyes heavy, jaw tight.

"Morning," she says.

He nods, not wasting syllables. His hair is doing a convincing impression of a failed Wi-Fi signal.

Alex closes the door behind her and moves to the desk. "I've been reviewing the JIRA tickets. One caught my eye. Something about base units of measure. I tried to follow the comments but got lost halfway through."

Sam leans back, rubs his face, and sighs like a man haunted by data ghosts. "You're talking about those ISO codes," he mutters. "They've caused more chaos than Brexit."

Alex tilts her head. A faint question mark is practically hovering above her.

He notices. "You look confused. Right, let's make this tangible."

He opens a drawer and pulls out two sealed packets of sticky notes. He holds them in each hand as evidence. He places one on the left, the other on the right of his keyboard.

He points to the left. "This sealed pack is a large box," he says, "Band of brothers. Kool and his Gang. Procurement uses large boxes to order in bulk."

"That makes sense," Alex smiles, "Cool…".

Then Sam picks up the other packet on the right and tears it open. The plastic snaps, sharp as a warning. Five small stacks in different colours spill out, and one almost dives straight into his coffee mug. "These individual suckers are small boxes. They are used in the warehouse for picking."

Sam looks at Alex. "Which one is the base unit?"

Alex points to the right. "These small 'suckers'," Alex replies, unsure of her answer.

"Correct. These small misfits need to be the base unit, as that is the smallest unit used in our company, in the warehouse." Sam gives Alex the seal of approval. "Keep that in mind. Because now you have to pay attention."

Alex narrows her eyes, as if that helps her concentrate more.

"In SAP, the platoon on the left carries the code LBX, and each rascal on the right goes by SBX. Five SBX rascals make one LBX platoon. Clear so far?"

Alex nods. "And SBX is the base unit."

"That's what you think…" Sam says slowly, a smile forming. "Here comes the interesting part." He lets an uncomfortable silence stretch, just long enough to build tension. "You agree that both LBX and SBX are boxes?"

"I guess so," Alex answers carefully, wondering if it's a trick question.

"Suppose, in the wonderful world of ISO codes, both LBX and SBX share the same ISO tag BX, for 'box'."

"Why would that make a difference?"

Sam's eyes light up, delighted by the question.

"Well, we use the SAP *Migrate Your Data* app to load data into S/4HANA. And this app only works with ISO codes. And you have to pick one SAP code as primary. LBX or SBX. All or nothing. Choose LBX as the primary by mistake, and every intended SBX instantly upgrades itself to an LBX. No arguments. No warning. Just enforced consistency at an industrial scale."

Alex blinks, jaw dropping as the penny hits. "O … my … God."

"Exactly, not 'Kool'. Imagine what happens in real life? Procurement thinks in bulk, an army of platoons, using code LBX, no problems there. However, the warehouse needs to pick up little buggers, our small boxes, but that becomes impossible. As LBX is marked as the *primary* for the BX ISO code during data migration, the smallest unit the warehouse can pick is a big box. It's like needing just one finger and only being able to get the full hand."

She blinks. "And they can't override it?"

"Nope. Once a single transaction hits that product with the wrong base unit, it's locked tighter than superglue. Instant. Permanently."

Alex presses her lips together. She can practically hear the project's timeline weeping. "That's… not ideal."

"Understatement of the century," Sam says dryly.

He gestures at the sticky notes. "This is what happens when ISO codes, those supposedly universal identifiers, turn into a trap. They're meant to make life easier, a shared language between systems and countries. But SAP can't handle ambiguity. It needs a single 'truth'. When two different SAP codes share one universal ISO code, it demands a favourite. Pick the wrong SAP code as the *primary* base unit, and you are cursed forever." Alex tries to process that. She can feel the migraine forming, somewhere behind the left eye.

"And this is not an isolated issue?" she wonders.

"No, impacts all departments. It's logistics, finance, manufacturing, all holding hands on a cliff edge."

Alex shakes her head. "Scary stuff." She exhales. "Let me try to say it back to you. Humour me."

Sam raises an eyebrow, intrigued.

"Last year, I was in Orlando," she begins. "Holiday. We went into a supermarket for one bottle of cola, the big two-litre kind. Only, in the States, they come shrink-wrapped in packs of six. I tried to take one out, and a shop assistant sprinted over like I'd attempted a robbery. Apparently, it's all or nothing. Six or none. The pack is sacred."

Sam smiles.

"Now imagine a European supermarket using that logic," she says. "The base unit becomes a pack of six bottles. Fine if you own a football team, a disaster if you just want one drink. You end up buying six colas when you only wanted one."

"Exactly that," Sam says. "Except instead of cola, we've got industrial materials. And our warehouse doesn't have a fridge big enough for this nonsense."

He grins, the first genuine grin she has seen from him. "You have just explained ISO confusion to the steering committee. They will hate it."

"Then it's perfect."

She gathers her notebook and turns to leave, then pauses to glance at the desk. Sticky notes lie scattered like casualties of process: one large pack, five small stacks, an entire governance failure in fluorescent paper.

As Alex reaches the door, Sam suggests, "Visit Jesse. He's got metaphors that make mine look optimistic."

Outside, the corridor feels too bright, the world suspiciously ordinary. Alex pauses, the metallic taste of recycled air still on her tongue, a mixture of flavours of systems that never rest. This isn't about codes or stationery; it's about how structure, once worshipped, outlives logic.

She opens her notebook and writes: *When it makes sense, it doesn't happen.*

Beneath it, smaller: *Fight for clarity, or chaos wins.*

Captain's Log: Commander To Base: Unit Is Raided

R – Risks / Root Causes

- SAP ISO codes exposed as the real trap.
- Two SAP codes share one ISO tag - instant chaos.
- Migration forced the wrong base unit (LBX over SBX).
- Wrong base unit now locked and untouchable.
- One wrong transaction froze the entire dataset.
- Governance illusion: structure outlived logic.

A – Actions

- Map all affected products and find the original unit choice.
- Confirm which departments depend on the wrong code.
- Use the cola-pack metaphor to explain the disaster simply.
- Enforce clarity and precision in documentation - no assumptions.
- Prepare evidence trail before escalation.

I – Impacts

- Warehouse cannot pick single units.
- Logistics, finance, and manufacturing all disrupted.
- Production simulations unreliable.
- Time and trust bleeding through the cracks.

D – Decisions / Dependencies

- Sam becomes the primary technical ally.
- Fight for absolute clarity, not comfort.
- Fix the data before touching process.
- Delay equals contamination.

Current state: **Early warning system activated.**

4: DIGGING IN
THE DIRT

Each step down the metal stairs echoes like a countdown to another problem. The corridor hums with hibernating air and the faint buzz of ageing servers. Somewhere, a fluorescent tube flickers, a nervous tic in light form. The air tastes of dust and regret. The dungeon sounds like a demotivational speaker. The stairs creak like they're charging overtime. She presses two fingers to her temple, trying to reboot clarity manually, and reminds herself there's a deadline attached to every breath.

Jesse's office is part cave, part battlefield. He is Sam's other half when it comes to data interrogation. Post-it notes curl on the walls like surrender flags, and reports lean in tired piles, paper edges bruised from use. Empty mugs form a defensive wall around his keyboard. A poster droops behind him, promising teamwork to whoever still believes in slogans. The monitor flickers, light carving trenches of focus and fatigue across his face. Shirt sleeves rolled to the elbow, he wears yesterday's stubble like a uniform; a pencil sits parked behind one ear and a pale coffee ring stains his cuff.

Alex pauses at the threshold, scanning bins stuffed with retired notes, a whiteboard sulking in half-erased bullet points, and cables coiled like tired snakes.

"Afternoon, Jesse," she says.

He looks up, eyes ringed but alert, fingers resting on the trackpad. "Afternoon. You look deep in thought."

"I am," she says. "I've just come from Sam. We pulled apart the SAP base-unit issues. I wanted to check it with you and hear what you think."

"Go on."

Her gaze snags on a few water bottles on the floor under his desk. One six-pack is still wrapped in plastic. She moves closer and points to it. "This is the problem we talked about. If the system treats a six-pack as the smallest unit, you can't pick one bottle."

Jesse nods. "I know. Sam told me at lunch about your Orlando supermarket kerfuffle. Unit-of-measure issues are ugly, the ISO-code mix-up is messy, but my problem right now is even scarier." He points to the bottles on the floor, neatly packed, then to the half-empty one on his desk. "To the eye, they look identical."

Alex examines the bottles. Same shape, same size. Then she twirls the half-full bottle on his desk and spots the difference. "They're not the same brand."

"That's it," he says. "Like twins. Now the million-dollar question: should they be treated differently?"

Alex frowns and takes a moment to think. "My gut says no. The brand shouldn't matter, as long as the bottles hold the same content and volume."

Jesse looks visibly delighted as he picks up the half-empty bottle. "I agree. Let's call this one Jekyll."

"Why?" Alex asks, puzzled.

"Because the six-pack *Hydes* under my desk," he says, triumphant, already too pleased with himself.

She laughs despite her rule never to encourage dad jokes.

He continues, "In our system, there's no need to keep Dr Jekyll and Mr Hyde apart when they're both two-litre water bottles. They should be one product. Unlucky for me, I have to scan through thousands of descriptions to find these multiple personalities."

He swivels to the screen and selects the **Descriptions** worksheet. The filter bar blinks. Columns narrow. Amber cells glow like warning lights. "Here you have the product descriptions in all languages. My challenge is to find 'Jekyll Plastic Water Bottle 2 Ltr' and 'XL Hyde Water Bottle' and somehow conclude they're the same thing."

"That's impossible," Alex says, her tone already admitting defeat.

"Exactly. That's why so many products end up duplicated after migration. I'm not the kind of person to throw in the towel that easily, so I need to do three things, in this order."

He stretches his arms, fingers flicking in mid-air like a conductor rehearsing an invisible orchestra.

"First, cleansing," he begins, "Fix the obvious wrongs in the raw data. Descriptions are the worst: typos, missing words, language slips, stray spaces. Make the fields comparable. You'd be surprised how many ways people misspell 'water'."

He filters a column and highlights rows in pairs. "Next, deduplication. Find our Jekylls and Hydes and mark them as the same person. I use a column called '*Match*' at the end to flag likely pairs."

Alex notices a lot of activity in that column and realises how many duplicates he's found. Then she spots another column further to the right.

Jesse keeps going. "Finally, this last column, '*Leader*'. That's what we call harmonisation. It means agreeing on one product as the basis for data migration."

"So, in our example we decide for every pair of Jekylls and Hydes whether we use Jekyll or Hyde as the leader for copying over the data during migration," Alex says, her tone brightening with confidence.

Jesse grins in approval.

She winces. "How bad is it overall?" already knowing the answer.

"Duplicates everywhere," he says. "Some dates missing, some codes misaligned. It's like a landfill out there. And this is just the product master data. We haven't even started with customers, suppliers and their addresses. That's an even worse minefield. Bad addresses delay deliveries and invoices. The cost is real."

He rubs the back of his neck, then stretches like a man untangling himself from the code. The chair squeaks, protesting the effort. Then he starts scrolling through the worksheet as if that alone could fix the mess.

Alex studies the screen, watching the endless rows flicker past. "And there's no tool that does this faster?"

Jesse chuckles. "In Excel? There are a hundred ways to find duplicates. COUNTIFs, filters, Power Query, you name it. You give this problem to Tom, Dick and Harry, you'll get different clever hacks and three different definitions of 'done'."

"So nothing standard," Alex says. "Everyone invents their own miracle."

"Pretty much. Excel rewards creativity, not consistency. Great for art, terrible for migration."

Alex folds her arms. "And your way... is it at least documented somewhere?"

Jesse gives her a look that's half amusement, half exhaustion. "When was the last time you had enough time for documentation?"

The silence that follows answers for both of them. The monitors hum. A column recalculates itself, quietly mocking them.

Finally Alex exhales. "So even the way we fix chaos is chaos."

"Welcome to the paradox," Jesse says. "We can harmonise data, but not the people cleaning it."

Alex leans against the desk, thinking aloud. "Maybe AI could do it. Copilot, or something like it. To spot the patterns, flag the duplicates, clean the mess automatically."

Jesse smirks. "Sure. Maybe it'll write the documentation and make coffee while it's at it."

She laughs. "So not quite ready for reality, then?"

"Let's say it's good at finding problems, not living with the consequences," he says, eyes back on the screen.

They both stare into the distance. Then Jesse breaks the impasse.

"Management loves Excel," he sighs. "Cheap hours, endless waste. The world's most popular software by accident. Now they treat AI like the sequel to the same old story, new name, same illusion. Mix the two, and you've got a double whammy."

He shakes his head. "Mark my words, top management will fall over themselves, convinced AI will fix everything. They force Tom, Dick and Harry to use AI-powered Excel and then wonder why the chaos just runs faster. Dehumanised, yes. Harmonised, never."

The joke lands flat but honest. She almost smiles. Sam's metaphors were messy; Jesse's are deadpan. Both true.

Her gaze tracks the rows marching toward oblivion, vanishing into the edges of his screen. The glow of the screen paints her reflection pale blue. "Just humour me for a second, and talk with me about solutions."

Jesse nods once. "Sure. We need a proper ETL tool. Extract, Transform, Load. Extract pulls data from the old systems. Transform cleans, finds duplicates, and harmonises everything into the shape the new system expects. Load is the final move into S/4HANA. The SAP *Migrate Your Data* app does the load very well, but it assumes the data is already clean. We miss speed and accuracy in the middle. It has a few transformation bits and pieces, yes, but not to the standard we need."

"So we're doing the Transform in Excel," she says, "which means every change is manual, slow, and hard to verify under pressure."

"Exactly," he says. "A proper ETL tool would handle cleansing rules, deduplication logic, and reliable checks. We could prove improvements by re-running the same set. With spreadsheets, we prove stamina, not quality."

"And you can't know for certain this ETL tool solves everything," Alex says. "So the new way of working can be easily dismissed as an overblown, all-singing, all-dancing solution with a price tag. It gives the 'better-the-Devil-you-know' AI-powered Excel the upper hand."

"That's how it plays," he says. "Meanwhile, we pay in evenings, eyeballs, and mistakes."

She taps a note into her tablet. "I'll take the argument upstairs. Stop pretending even AI-fuelled Excel excels and start buying accuracy with a proper tool. Call it an investment in fewer defects, fewer reworks, and shorter test cycles. Hard to model perfectly, but honest."

"AI can hallucinate faster than humans can verify," he says. "We need to stop pretending it saves time or replaces oversight."

Jesse stares at his terminal. "Let's get back to reality and fix what actually breaks in the load. Here's what I need. Short term. The time of democracy is over. I need a single business owner who takes responsibility and approves matches and leaders. I can spot them, but someone from the business has to agree. A second opinion with an instant seal of approval. Not a committee, a person who signs off."

Alex nods. "You want the business to take ownership. I can get that moving."

"And I want it written down," Jesse adds. "One page. So when someone asks why we're not 'just loading,' we point to the rules."
"Agreed," she says. "We have a plan. That counts for something."

She stands, the chair sighing with relief. The hallway outside glows dim under tired lights. Her reflection follows her in the glass, a woman set on cleaning data and conscience at the same time.

She pauses at the metal stairs before going up. The hum of hibernating air still clings to the walls, heavier now that she knows what's buried beneath them. She glances back. Jesse hunches over the keyboard, shoulders drawn up like brackets holding the whole system together. The monitor's cold light gives him a ghost-engineer glow. Persistence in human form.

He's not lazy. Just outnumbered.

Captain's Log: A Raider Is Not A Twix

R – Risks / Root Causes

- Duplicates are everywhere - no single version of truth.
- Product descriptions inconsistent across systems.
- Bad addresses delaying deliveries and invoices.
- Excel encourages creative cleansing - each version its own gospel.
- Management still betting on flawed spreadsheets as strategy.

A – Actions

- Assign one named business owner to approve all "matches" and "leaders."
- End cleansing by committee - ownership or nothing.
- Document formal cleansing rules; make them visible.
- Build the business case for a proper ETL tool.
- Challenge the "AI-powered Excel" myth before it spreads.

I – Impacts

- Cleansing slow, manual, and error-prone.
- Bad data blocking operations and billing.
- Defects and rework costs climbing daily.
- Human inconsistency locking system progress.

D – Decisions / Dependencies

- Jesse confirmed as data clean-up lead.
- Secure a single business sign-off authority.
- Push for ETL investment - accuracy over speed.
- Stop selling miracles; start proving precision.

Current state: **Structure drafted, politics loading.**

5: POLITICS BY CANDLELIGHT

Thursday night, and the Riverside Club terrace glitters with small talk and fake smiles, an ecosystem powered by temperamental broadband and warm white wine. Success smells of citrus polish and guarded laughter. Candlelight glints off glassware, too romantic for a corporate celebration. Conversations hum like servers running on charm.

Alex does not want to be here. The navy dress she chose this morning had felt safe. Now it just feels like armour: neat, unadorned, designed to blend in. Richard's twenty-year-in-service celebration has too few guests for her to hide. After Tuesday's showdown, skipping tonight would only prove she cracked. Time for her to put on the fake thick skin. Turn up, smile, be seen, then slip out through the back door. That is the plan. She has already ticked *congratulate Richard* off her mental checklist, one polite smile delivered, duty done. All that remains is to finish her drink and make a clean escape.

She lingers by the terrace rail, city lights flickering on the river like data points searching for alignment. She can still see Sam and Jesse hunched over their spreadsheets, eyes red from polishing data by hand, making the gloss here feel fictional. Jesse's message is clear: stop doing surgery with Excel, buy a tool that cleans before you load. If she can get the right person to back it, she has a shot at making actual progress.

A burst of applause rolls out from the main room. On the screen inside, Richard's picture beams out, tuxedo pressed and cufflinks catching the projector light, the smile of a man who never looks off duty. People drift toward the speeches. Alex stays in the cooler air, watching the minutes collapse into seconds.

Perfume and ambition arrive first. Claire glides into view in a silver sheath that catches every stray light, scarf tied like a signature. Her hair and posture have board approval written all over them, her smile composed for cameras and crises.

"Enjoying the evening?" Her tone slides between silk and scalpel, smooth enough to soothe, sharp enough to score.

"Lovely," Alex says, voice steady. "Congratulations to Richard."

There it is, the opening move.

"How is the one-week deadline?" Claire asks, swirling her wine as if it holds the truth.

"Challenging," Alex replies. "It is a puzzle." Every word is reconnaissance. Stay calm and composed, Alex.

Claire's smile is almost kind. "Not every piece fits, does it?"

"Eventually it will," Alex says, meeting her gaze. A tightness flickers at the corner of Claire's mouth, the faintest crack in perfection.

Alex does not waste the opportunity. "I want to put something on the table. We need an ETL tool. Extract, Transform, Load. The transform bit is the boring part that cleans and standardises data before you put it in the system. Right now we load too quickly, but we don't clean or correct properly, which is why mistakes keep sneaking into the testing system."

Claire tilts her head, empathy patented, glamour certified. "ETL?" she repeats, tasting the acronym more than understanding it.

"Yes," Alex says. "Jesse walked me through it. He's stuck with Excel and nobody to validate the data. We need clear rules and a way to apply them, so we can find bad data fast without spending nights eyeballing spreadsheets."

"Richard is focused on deadlines," Claire replies. Her glass catches the terrace light. "We do not have time to introduce new tooling."

Alex nods slowly. Claire wants to dodge tooling. Let's see how she handles accountability. "Then we also need someone to own the data. End users have to be accountable for quality before anything gets loaded. Right now they throw files at the IT team and walk away like it's someone else's mess."

Claire's expression stills, the kind of calm that warns more than it soothes. "Ownership," she says lightly, "is a governance discussion. It sits under my area."

"Then take it," Alex says, voice edged with a bite. The words are quiet but hit like impact. "Because without owners, no tool in the world will fix this."

Claire's smile hardens. "Let us not confuse accountability with delivery. The business already has enough on its plate. Leave the politics to me, Alex."

"It is not politics," Alex says. "It is responsibility."

"And responsibility," Claire replies, her tone smooth as polished sapwood, "is all about knowing your limits."

Another round of cheers drifts through the doors. Someone toasts tenure. Claire glances back, as if the celebration belongs to her, the smile returning as she faces Alex again. "If you are that worried about responsibility, talk to Morgan in data ops. She is obsessed with post-load fixes. You two will have plenty to discuss."

Alex studies her. The name lands like a lifeline wrapped in condescension.

"Noted," she says.

Claire's eyes narrow just enough to show satisfaction. "Always happy to help," she replies, and turns back toward the noise inside.

Behind Alex, a pocket of laughter spikes, the warm sound of people who believe that milestones cure problems.

Alex places the empty glass on the marble table that feels cool under her fingers, a reminder that warmth here is decorative. Through the window she catches Claire beside Richard, leaning close, lips moving in a low current of words. Richard nods once, expression unreadable, the kind of slow agreement that never bodes well.

Alex's stomach tightens. She tells herself it could be anything, but her imagination fills the blanks faster than reason can stop it. She can almost hear her name shaped between them, another problem discussed under candlelight. She looks away and forces her focus back to what she can control.

She can help Sam and Jesse. On Tuesday, she will put their struggles in front of the room where it belongs. Alex wants to solve problems, but maybe, for now, the best she can do is tell the truth about them. And maybe Morgan can add a contribution as well, something concrete to prove how deep the issue runs.

She checks her watch. She reminds herself: be seen, then slip away into the night. She looks around. Nobody notices her. Time to go, before sincerity ruins the evening.

She turns and fixes on the EXIT sign above the lush double doors. For Alex, it looks like an escape hatch. She makes her move towards freedom, each step lighter than the last.

"Leaving so soon?"

Richard's voice carries easily over the applause, calm and deliberate. He steps into the hallway, glass in hand, blocking her path, his smile composed to the millimetre.

"Big week ahead," he says. "I trust you will have something concrete for us on Tuesday."

"That is the plan," Alex replies, matching his tone.

"Good." He takes a small step closer, lowering his voice just enough to cut through the noise. "Some of the executive board will be joining. They want assurance this project is under control."

Her pulse stumbles. It feels as if someone has pulled the floor from under her feet. "Understood."

Richard notices, of course. His mouth twitches, then smooths back into discipline.

"I do not need promises, Alex," he says. "I need proof. No surprises.

No improvisation. Keep it tight."

Each word lands like a controlled strike. She gathers herself and meets his gaze.

"You will have it."

He nods once, satisfied. "I am counting on that."

For a moment his eyes search hers, steady, clinical, as if decoding her thoughts. Then he turns back towards the room and is gone, absorbed by polite laughter and the renewed buzz of conversation, leaving Alex alone in the quiet. His words remain where they hit, cold and precise, sprayed across her mind like corporate graffiti.

Captain's Log: Diplomacy Raid Completed, Barely Surviving

R – Risks / Root Causes

- Claire rejected the ETL proposal, dodging accountability.
- Executive board joining Tuesday's review - visibility high, tolerance low.
- Richard demands proof, not promises.
- Data ownership still politically radioactive.
- Personal pressure at critical level.

A – Actions

- Find Morgan in Data Ops - she knows post-load failures inside out.
- Gather evidence from her logs as hard proof.
- Prepare factual case for Tuesday's review - no theatre, just truth.
- Force business ownership back into the spotlight.
- Align Jesse's and Sam's findings for unified story.

I – Impacts

- Data quality debate now fully political.
- Accountability pushed aside for optics.
- One-week deadline confirmed as immovable.
- My credibility rides on Tuesday's results.

D – Decisions / Dependencies

- Richard's trust equals survival.
- Morgan is potential new ally - technical and moral.
- Fear wastes time; clarity buys control.
- Manage the message, own the outcome.

Current state: **Overpromise: Check.**

6: OLD HABITS NEVER DIE

The air in the data room feels pressurised. Servers hum like insomniacs, screens blink in tired rhythm and the smell of burnt circuits clings to the carpet. Fluorescent light flattens everything into shades of paperwork grey. Coffee cups cluster on desks like a defensive wall. The room runs on caffeine and irony.

Alex stops at the doorway and breathes in the hum. A faint chill seeps from the air vents, doing its best to cool the heat of frustration. She rolls her sleeves, notebook under one arm, and steps inside.

Morgan loads our data into SAP. She sits in front of three monitors, one headphone dangling, hair pulled into a loose bun pinned with a pencil. The blue light from the screens turns her olive skin metallic, catching the faint silver threads at her temples. A pair of narrow glasses rest low on her nose, sliding forward whenever she leans in. Her black hoodie is flecked with lint and faint coffee stains, the uniform of someone who has stopped pretending to care about dress codes. Her dark hazel eyes flick between lines of code, sharp but calm, the kind of calm built from long exposure to chaos.

Without looking up, she says, "What disaster are we entertaining today?"

Morgan pushes her glasses back up with an ink-smudged finger, eyes narrowing at the screen before softening again. The gesture is habitual, unhurried. The rhythm of someone who has survived too many deadlines to waste energy on panic.

"The kind that refuses to go away," Alex replies.

Morgan tilts her head towards the screens. "Legacy loads again. Same data, new flavour. They hand us expired milk and lumpy flour, then want a Michelin dessert."

Alex smiles faintly. "So, the recipe is fine. The ingredients are rotten."

"Exactly. The joy of enterprise systems," Morgan mutters. "The business insists IT broke the mapping. IT insists the business can't type. Meanwhile, the system just sits there judging us all."

Alex leans forward. "Show me."

Morgan opens the latest error log. Lines of red glare back at them. "This one's my favourite. 'Field not recognised.' It means something's wrong but it refuses to say what. Classic passive aggression."

Alex scans the page. "How's *Migrate Your Data* behaving?"

Morgan chuckles without humour. "The app behaves like a factory with no repair shop. It creates, but it can't update. Once data is loaded incorrectly, you're on your own."

Alex frowns. "If it can only create, we're fixing chaos too late. Why not clean it before the data is extracted from the old systems?"

Morgan looks up for the first time, lips quirking. "That's the dream. Talk to Greg. If anyone knows how S/4HANA gets fed, it's him."

Alex notes the name in her book but keeps quiet.

Morgan turns back to her screens. "Meanwhile, we've got LSMW and mass updates. Both are dangerous."

She adds a dramatic pause, scanning Alex to recognise more detail is needed.

"Still hiding in plain sight in S/4HANA, SAP doesn't support the prehistoric migration tool LSMW anymore but people resurrect it whenever they want nostalgia. And mass updates? One wrong filter and every product in high demand goes on sale for reasons nobody remembers."

"Mass updates give efficiency with the occasional collateral damage," Alex says.

"Exactly. Fast, blind, fatal. I once changed a thousand records instead of ten. Spent the rest of the day pretending it was planned."

Alex grins. "Manual updates might be safer."

Morgan shakes her head. "Not when you're so tired you type 'yes' instead of 'no'. Romantic precision, quickly followed by regret. So time to revive LSMW, like Frankenstein's monster."

They both laugh, the brittle sound of shared survival.

Alex glances around. The room is small and windowless, walls lined with whiteboards that have lost the will to stay clean. A fan buzzes near the ceiling, pushing the stale air in circles. Stacks of archive boxes guard the door. Someone has taped a yellow sticky note to one: *Do Not Touch Unless You're Braver Than Me.*

"So we're relying on a relic and call it progress," Alex says, "praying it does not fall apart."

"Move along, nothing to see here…" Morgan replies, sipping coffee from a chipped mug that reads *Trust Me, I'm a Data Engineer.*

Alex studies the glow from the monitors, blue reflections pulsing across Morgan's face. "What would actually make this easier?"

"A real ETL tool," Morgan says.

"Interesting. I heard that before," Alex says.

Morgan glances at her screen. "But we don't have such a tool. We are stuck with the *Migrate Your Data* app. And insult to injury, this SAP app runs on Excel templates. You can't escape them. The app drags you right back in."

Her phone buzzes, then stops, satisfied with the distraction it caused. Morgan pretends to ignore it, but takes a moment to gather her thoughts.

"And you can't even tame the template," she adds. "SAP locks it down like sacred scripture: same tabs, same columns, same pain.

feeding its holy spreadsheet exactly as written and pray it doesn't smite us."

"So *Migrate Your Data* creates but cannot change, not even the structure it demands," Alex recaps. "Mass updates risk disaster. LSMW is ancient. The only real fix is before the load, inside a spreadsheet that feels like a straitjacket."

Morgan points at her with her pencil. "You said it. Start loading bad data and you'll spend eternity cleansing after the fact, not before it. The world upside down."

"Sounds very efficient," Alex says.

"Say that to Greg," Morgan repeats. "Not sure whether he will laugh or cry."

Alex smiles. "Encouraging."

Morgan's laugh is dry. "Encouragement is above my pay grade."

Alex closes her notebook and looks around again. The room hums, alive with activity but drained of energy. Coffee fumes mix with the metallic tang of overworked machines. A stack of cables snakes along the skirting board, one frayed enough to make safety officers weep.

She stands and mumbles, "All right, you make sense. If only I could get some evidence to convince Richard."

She's halfway to the door when Morgan calls, "Wait! The change log in S/4HANA."

Alex turns. "What about it?"

"It tracks every field change. Who changed what and when. Like a flight recorder for data."

"A black box for chaos," Alex says.

"Exactly. If we use it properly, we can see which fields keep breaking, who keeps touching them, and how many times we reload the same rubbish."

Alex's eyebrows lift. "Evidence instead of guesswork."

Morgan nods. "Let me dig into this log and see if I can give you some statistics. By Monday morning, OK for you?”

Alex laughs quietly. “Richard will be overjoyed if you can manage that.”

“I’ll make it so.”

“I owe you one,” Alex replies and glances at the clock. Time melts again. The servers hum steadily, lights blinking like thoughts refusing to stop.

“Thanks, Morgan,” she says. “Lifesaver with a lightsabre.”

“Sure. Call me Obi-Wan,” Morgan says, smiling, half amusement, half fatigue.

Alex moves to the exit. The glass door reflects the room behind her: Morgan hunched over the monitors, sleeves rolled to her elbows, the glow outlining her profile like a halo made of code. The servers thrum in low harmony, indifferent but constant.

The corridor feels too bright, the air thin after the mechanical hum.

Alex opens her notebook. Greg’s name is circled, the ink pressed deep. *Migrate Your Data* can build but it can’t heal. The cure starts where the data begins.

She closes the book, lifts her chin, and walks. The machines fade behind her, but the rhythm follows, steady as intent. Time still runs against her, but now it finally has coordinates.

Captain's Log: Join The Raid With Obi-Wan

R – Risks / Root Causes

- *Migrate Your Data* creates but cannot correct.
- Its Excel templates are fixed - columns and tabs locked like sacred text
- Legacy tool **LSMW** still revived for shortcuts - risky nostalgia.
- **Mass updates** offer speed with collateral damage.
- One wrong filter could wipe a department before lunch.
- Cleansing after load equals endless rework.
- Old habits still migrating freely under new names.

A – Actions

- Shift focus: fix issues **before** the load, not after.
- Speak with **Greg** - understand how S/4HANA gets its data.
- Morgan to extract **change-log statistics** by Monday.
- Use log output as factual proof for Richard.
- Frame findings as cost of bad habits versus cost of proper tooling.

I – Impacts

- Manual correction cycles draining time and energy.
- Excel-driven updates sustaining systemic errors.
- Evidence now within reach - measurable by change-log data.
- For once, progress has coordinates.

D – Decisions / Dependencies

- **Morgan** delivering log report = first tangible proof.
- **Greg** next key source for upstream investigation.
- Present evidence to Richard early next week.

- ETL tool remains long-term target; credibility depends on Monday's data.

Current state: **Evidence incoming, morale cautiously functional.**

7. CONFUSE AND RULE

Morgan is right. If anyone knows how bad data actually finds its way into *Migrate Your Data*, it is Greg, the business data lead. He is the nerve centre for our migration. He collects inputs from every department, merges them, and guards the data like a nightclub bouncer on a deadline.

The open-plan office hums like a tired circuit board, its lights running on habit and denial. Rows of screens present countless spreadsheets like digital wallpaper. Every desk is an island of notes, empty mugs, and survival snacks. The carpet underfoot is worn flat by chair wheels. Somewhere a printer rattles, then surrenders.

Alex follows the sound of relentless keyboard taps until she spots him at the far end. Greg sits in a fortress of monitors, the glow outlining his broad shoulders and salt-and-pepper hair. His dark skin catches the light, the silver at his temples glinting like solder on a circuit board. Reading glasses perch halfway down his nose, framing eyes ringed with the soft red of long hours. A short, neatly trimmed goatee shadows his jaw, the colour of graphite against tired skin. A cracked mug sits on a pile of printouts titled *HOPE*.

"Greg?" she says.

He does not look up. "Give me a second. Excel is thinking."

The screen refreshes, a ripple of amber cells blinking across columns. He exhales through his nose, quiet but heavy, the sound of someone who has buried too many versions of the same file. He presses the bridge of his nose where the glasses have left small dents, a reflex carved by years of screens and deadlines.

Alex drops her notebook onto the desk beside him. "Morgan said you're the one feeding *Migrate Your Data* with extracted data from the old systems"

That earns a faint smile. "Feeding is generous. I shovel."

She leans in. "Mind if I look?"

"Help yourself. Just don't expect it to behave."

The spreadsheet fills the screen, the number of worksheets surpassing the horizon, columns within the open worksheet are endless, cells colour-coded like a risk assessment gone wrong. Comment boxes dangle like warning signs. Something about the layout feels familiar. The frozen panes. The formatting. Even the sarcastic note in column G: *DO NOT TOUCH UNLESS YOU HATE YOURSELF.*

Alex frowns. "Hold on. Is this the *Product Load* file?"

Greg finally looks up, eyebrows raised above his glasses. "You've met it?"

"Are Sam, Jesse and Morgan also trying to fix this exact sheet. You're all wrestling the same monster."

He lets out a short laugh, more sigh than amusement. "Maybe that explains the disappearing formulas."

For a moment they stare at the screen, as that alone solves the murder scene.

"Walk me through what you do here," she says.

Greg rubs his eyes, then gestures to the spreadsheet. "I extract, collect and supervise. Then Sales completes missing descriptions, Finance reviews stock valuations, and Production verifies planning data. Everyone contributes their piece. Nobody owns the whole thing."

"Sounds democratic," she says.

"Democracy's fine until it votes against logic." He scrolls, the spreadsheet flickering like a restless heartbeat. "Think of it as a puzzle. I'm the one who opens the box, dumps the pieces on the table, and groups them roughly by colour. Then the departments take over. Sales paints the sky, Finance builds the houses, Production lays the roads. Everyone's proud of their bit, but nobody checks the grey areas, the space where the sky is supposed to meet the houses and roads. We end up with a perfect mess and no accountability."

Alex frowns. "So who deals with the grey areas?"

"Guilty as charged. I'm the data lead, responsible for putting the puzzle together. My job's to connect the dots and find the missing pieces hiding in plain sight."

He rubs the back of his neck, silver hair catching the light. His glasses slip down again, and he leaves them there. He doesn't need to see clearly to know what a mess looks like.

"How long has this file been alive?"

"Longer than some careers." He points at the file name. "*FINAL_v9. We started it during the template phase. Since then, it's been copied, merged, duplicated, lost, found and finally corrupted. It's digital inbreeding."

He clicks another tab. "We keep it on a shared drive. Half the team edits online, half offline. Someone forgets to close it, and Excel panics. No version control. No audit trail. It's organised disobedience with management blessing."

Alex studies the sheet. Rows shift beneath her cursor, numbers flickering like anxious thoughts. "So every morning you pray it's still there, the way you left it the night before. Then you rebuild order in the morning and chaos restores itself by lunch."

"Always the optimist," he says.

She watches him work, hands steady but slow. The fatigue lives in the pauses, not the gestures.

"Why not assign ownership?" she asks.

"We tried. Everyone volunteered someone else."

Alex smirks. "Classic."

Greg shrugs. "Ownership means risk. When things go wrong, people prefer to look busy instead of responsible."

Cells blink. A column resizes itself. A pale green highlight slides across the screen as if guided by an invisible hand.

Greg sighs without looking up. "Look who we have here... our ghost editor."

The cursor freezes, then the BS initials jump again. Alex feels the same low chill she had in Sam's office. Systems changing themselves while everyone pretends control exists.

"You know," she says, "this file is a single point of failure. Accidentally copy and paste wrong and…"

"Boom," Greg finishes. "A week gone, no clue whose version was right."

"Efficient," she says.

"We call it Agile," he replies, mouth curving into that tired smirk that only data people understand.

He pushes his glasses up with a forefinger, the gesture automatic, then leans back, chair creaking, gaze on the ceiling tiles stained from old leaks. "Funny thing is, the more we lean into Excel, the worse the process gets. I've written governance guides thicker than a 1980s monitor, but nobody reads them. The spreadsheet does not care. No scruples at all."

They share a short silence, the hum of the office threading between them.

"What would ownership look like?" she asks.

Greg thinks for a moment. "One name. One person who signs off before anything moves. Someone who can say 'yes' without looking for the nearest exit. Control, Alt, Escape."

He gestures at the screens. "Even the columns play along. '**Match**' and '**Leader**' are good ideas from Jesse. Then three departments want the crown. Sales wants data from A, Finance from B, and Production from C. All the same product, just different codes for different teams. Who becomes the leader? Everyone and no one. A perfect Mexican stand-off."

She studies him. No self-pity, only pragmatic exhaustion. Greg is not chaos. He is alignment trapped in the wrong structure.

"You realise," she says, "you, Sam, Jesse and Morgan are describing the same problem. Fix errors nobody owns."

Greg glances at her, eyes bright behind tired lenses. "That makes us colleagues or victims?"

"Both," she says. "But at least now we know what the crime is."

They smile, not out of joy but recognition.

Alex looks at her notebook. "What will we tell Richard?"

"That we don't have a data problem. We have an ownership problem," Greg says, his voice firm but weary. "And good luck selling that. I'll be hiding behind the curtains with a bag of popcorn."

Alex laughs, genuine this time.

For a moment the fluorescent light seems almost kind as she leaves the room.

In the corridor she pauses and writes in her notebook: *Same spreadsheet. Many hands. No owner. Everyone fits their piece of the sky. Some pieces get lost.*

She stares into space, the thought widening by the second, and adds one more line: *Find the person who sees the whole picture.*

Captain's Log: All Cells Raided, None Trusted

R – Risks / Root Causes

- The **Product Load file** is the single point of failure.
- Corrupted spreadsheet relic - no version control, no audit trail.
- Data edited by too many hands; ghost changes everywhere.
- Endless copies causing digital inbreeding.
- Process looks structured but runs on denial.

A – Actions

- Freeze all edits in the master sheet until ownership defined.
- Identify the single **Leader** for data sign-off.
- End the departmental Mexican stand-off - one owner, one truth.
- Support **Greg** in rejecting unverified updates.
- Document control rules before another "final v9" appears.

I – Impacts

- Process democratic, not logical - chaos by consensus.
- Everyone contributes; no one owns the outcome.
- Errors regenerate faster than they're fixed.
- Cleansing effort erased daily by re-uploads.

D – Decisions / Dependencies

- Same spreadsheet. No owner. No control.
- The real failure is an **ownership problem**, not a data problem.
- Must find the person who sees the **whole picture**.
- Prepare to brief Richard with the unpopular truth.

- **Greg** = alignment trapped in the wrong structure.

Current state: **Control pending, patience expired.**

8. STILL HAVING THE FOGGIEST

A brittle twig snaps beneath Alex's boot. Each step cracks through silence like bad code. Frost clings to roots. The forest smells of pine and clean decay this Saturday morning while light filters through the canopy in thin, patient lines. She exhales, breath drifting away into the chill.

Her husband, Steve, walks half a step behind. His calm trails her like insulation against noise. He's in his early forties, shoulders broad from quiet strength rather than gym ambition, brown eyes steady behind the glasses. His jumper smells faintly of aftershave and cold air. Even the forest seems to copy his rhythm, steady and unhurried. A few grey strands catch the light as he adjusts his pace to match hers.

"You've been grinding your teeth since we left," he says.

Does she? Lately her jaw does more work than her team. "Occupational hazard."

"Still carrying the project?"

"Our data migration approach is built on wishful thinking," she says. "That SAP app with the clever name, *Migrate Your Data*, overpromises and underdelivers."

Her boot catches frozen mud. "We thought it was the complete package. It forces you to use Excel, and those templates are too complex for even seasoned experts. I don't even want to bore you with all the details. But it paves a scenic route through hell."

"Maybe hell just needed a better tour guide," he says, sleeves rolled to the forearm, charcoal jumper frayed.

She half-smiles. "You volunteering?"

"Not today."

"The app can't handle transformation properly," she says. "It accepts junk disguised as industry standard."

Steve stays quiet, the look on his face saying enough.

"Morgan says this app creates data but can't repair it. Jesse's drowning in duplicates. Sam's fighting base units that make no sense. Everyone guards a corner of the puzzle but no one looks up."

Steve stops walking, making Alex turn. His breath clouds the air, a hint of stubble softening the edges of a face built for patience.

He smiles. "And you?"

"I'm the idiot in a dark room with only a flashlight." She laughs quietly. "I need a light switch to see the whole picture."

He smirks. "Enlightening."

They walk in quiet rhythm, boots cracking frost. A crow complains overhead. Pines march in straight rows beside a dip towards unseen water. Above, sunlight stitches holes in the canopy and turns dust to glitter.

Steve smiles. "When no one looks up, maybe you're the one who needs to look down. Look for breadcrumbs."

"Breadcrumbs?"

"Small clues. Collect enough of them and you'll start to see paths on a map. What if Sam, Jesse, Morgan, and Greg are all islands, and your job is to build the bridges?"

She frowns. "You make it sound so easy. And who's cleaning the mess? Probably me." She sighs, the words heavier than she expects.

Steve glances sideways. "You're not the cleaner, Alex. You're the architect. Your job is to make sure the right people and tools hold the shovels. If you start digging, you'll never finish the map."

She laughs softly. "Delegation, not penance."

"Exactly. Draw the map. Lead the clean-up, don't join the dig."

They reach a weathered wooden bench overlooking a shallow valley where mist hangs between the trees. Alex sits first, shoulders loosening as the cold wood grounds her. Steve joins her, elbows on his knees, watching the light slide across the hills. For a minute neither of them speaks. The silence feels earned.

"It's quiet here," she says.

"That's why I like it," he replies. "On a good day you can see for miles."

She nods, watching the fog slide through the valley, matching the haze still hanging in her thoughts.

They rise and follow the path down towards the stream. Water slides over stones, clear and cold. The current hums like an idea finding tempo. She crouches and touches the surface. The chill bites her fingertips but clears her head. Branches, sky and reflection merge into a single image. She tilts her head, unaware she's seeing the whole picture she's been chasing.

"You ever notice," Steve says, "how you talk like someone who knows the way out without realising?"

She laughs. "My head's still foggy."

"Fog clears eventually, and clarity reveals itself."

They stand together, watching the water shift around stones. The forest runs on its own logic. No dashboards. No deadlines. Only flow.

"You think it's salvageable?" she asks.

He considers. "The mess, yes. The people, definitely. Perfection, never. But perfection is a terrible metric anyway."

"Progress, not perfection," she repeats. The phrase fits like a file that finally loads.

The path softens to mud. The air warms, scented with pine and thawing wood. Sunlight touches her neck, and the chill leaves her hands.

"For the first time in weeks, I'm not angry," she says.

The light turns gold and scatters across wet moss, bright as a reset button. Alex stops and watches it. The world feels less like a problem and more like a solution waiting to be discovered.

"Ready to head back?" Steve asks.

"Yes. We both deserve a hot chocolate." She looks once more at the clearing where every line of light finds its place. "Everything might fit. I just need to see it."

Steve smiles. "One step at a time."

Alex nods. "And this time, I will."

Captain's Log: Raiding For Crumbs

R – Risks / Root Causes

- Current data approach built on **wishful thinking**.
- *Migrate Your Data* app **overpromises** and underdelivers.
- Excel templates too complex, forcing expert bottlenecks.
- Everyone sees only their **own corner of the puzzle**.

A – Actions

- Stop joining the dig - cleaning isn't leadership.
- My role is the **architect**, not the cleaner.
- **Draw the map** linking Sam, Jesse, Morgan, Greg.
- **Delegate** the penance; guide the structure.
- Focus on **progress, not perfection**.

I – Impacts

- I've been the **idiot with a flashlight** instead of the one building the grid.
- Exhaustion comes from fixing symptoms, not systems.
- The fog hides the pattern - I need the light switch, not another torch.
- The system's salvageable; perfection isn't the goal.

D – Decisions / Dependencies

- Follow the **breadcrumbs** - every clue leads to the bigger picture.
- Use team findings as **bridges**, not islands.
- Clarity will surface if I lead, not chase.
- Restore direction - and balance - before the next storm.

Current state: **Recharged with hot chocolate.**

9. KITCHEN WAR ROOM

A spoon clatters into the sink, a small metallic protest against another working Sunday. Alex tells herself she will stop doing this one day, but promises never last. The hum of the fridge sounds like quiet judgement. The smell of garlic and rosemary thickens the air. Cassoulet again, Steve's therapy of choice. The old oak table fills the middle of the kitchen, its surface marked by years of family dinners and late-night deadlines. Rain freckles the window and blurs the hedgerow outside.

Steve stands at the sink, rinsing beans with monk-like calm. He moves with the slow rhythm of someone who trusts process over panic. He is the still point to her constant spin, the reminder that structure and breath matter more than speed. The lamp over the stove paints his hair with warm light.

Alex drops her bag on a chair and opens her notebook. From it, she pulls out a single pack of sticky notes split into five colours. Yellow, pink, blue, green, and a band of bright orange at the end. She tears away the plastic, the faint static snapping in the air, and almost tips her wine glass in the process. "Back to the drawing board for one last time," she murmurs.

Steve glances over his shoulder.

She flips through her pages, reading fragments from weeks that feel like years. Then she writes endless notes, sticking them to the table in no particular order.

- *Sam: Two SAP codes share one ISO tag - instant chaos.*

- *Sam: Governance illusion: structure outlived logic.*
- *Jesse: Duplicates are everywhere - no single version of truth.*
- *Jesse: Excel encourages creative cleansing - each version its own gospel.*
- *Morgan: Migrate Your Data creates but cannot correct.*
- *Greg: The Product Load file is the single point of failure.*
- *Greg: Same spreadsheet. No owner. No control.*
- *Hubby: Everyone sees only their own corner of the puzzle.*

Alex stares at the notes, and a memory flashes-the blinking cells, the ghost in the sheet, Greg's muttered disbelief. She sees it replay in her mind. Everyone describes the same kind of pain with different words. They all work in the same cursed spreadsheet. A recipe for disaster.

She laughs under her breath. "BS."

Steve looks over. "What?"

"In Greg's office," she says, still half laughing. "The spreadsheet started editing itself. Cells flashing, columns resizing, and these initials-BS-kept popping up. No one knew who it was. Half the company was in there at once, fixing and breaking things at the same time."

Steve smirks. "BS, huh? That feels symbolic."

"Exactly. The file isn't haunted," Alex says, grinning. "It is just full of actual BS-people editing over each other, pretending it is control."

Steve chuckles, shaking his head. "So your colleagues behave as their own worst enemies."

"Pretty much," she says. "And this fake sense of control keeps us out of control."

They laugh together, the sound cutting through the rain outside. The humour makes the point land hard. Too many hands, one file, and a system littered with manure.

She writes it on a fresh orange note: *Same spreadsheet = same failure.*

Steve turns off the gas and rests a hand on the counter. "So Excel's your battlefield," he says. "If that file's the crime scene, who's the forensic lead?"

Alex lifts her pen again. Who indeed. She flicks through her notes for clues and some light up.

- *Sam: Map all affected products and find the original unit choice.*
- *Jesse: Document formal cleansing rules; make them visible.*
- *Morgan: Fix issues before the load, not after.*
- *Greg: Errors regenerate faster than they're fixed.*

She lays the new notes across the table in a line.

Steve dries his hands and leans over the table. "Sam chases patterns, Jesse plays janitor, Morgan patches the damage, and Greg keeps the lights on."

Alex smiles. "That's the project in one sentence."

Other notes catch her attention.

- *Greg: Must find the person who sees the whole picture.*
- *Jesse: End cleansing by committee - ownership or nothing.*

The two sentences belong together. Greg already acts as the custodian. He just doesn't have permission to own it.

"Greg's the one," she says. "He's already doing the job."

Steve nods. "Keeper of the monster."

"One custodian, one truth," she replies. She presses a green note on top of the others.

The scent of the cassoulet fills the room. For a brief moment, the world feels ordered.

Then Steve speaks again. "If he's extracting and loading in the same file, isn't he still fighting the same war?"

Alex stops mid-note. The question lands hard. He's right. Nothing changes if the battlefield stays the same. She scans her notebook for confirmation.

- *Jesse: Assign one named business owner to approve all*

> *matches and leaders.*
> - *Claire: Data ownership still politically radioactive.*
> - *Greg: Freeze all edits in the master sheet until ownership defined.*
> - *Better Half: Use team findings as bridges, not islands.*

She keeps reading, waiting for something to connect. The pattern is close; she can feel it, but it still hides in plain sight. Her finger rests on Greg's note. *Freeze all edits in the master sheet until ownership defined.*

Steve leans on the counter. "Tell me about this master sheet. What's actually in it?"

"It's one monster file," Alex says. "A gazillion worksheets. Every department has at least one tab, sometimes more. And every tab has more columns than sense. Most of them are blank. I doubt half the people even know what the headers mean."

Steve nods, drying his hands with a tea towel. "So all those empty cells just sit there, doing nothing. Isn't that… noise?"

She hesitates. "Noise, yes, but we can't touch it. The *Migrate Your Data* tool issues the template. We're supposed to fill it exactly as it is. Removing columns is out of the question."

"Aren't rules made to be broken?"

"Not these ones," she says, defensive out of habit.

Steve raises an eyebrow. "Then make your own rules."

Alex opens her mouth, then stops. The penny hovers, refusing to drop. If most of those columns are pointless, then the problem isn't the people filling them. It is the template itself.

She hears his words again. *Make your own rules.*

He shrugs. "At the extract stage, why not pull only what matters? Let each department have its own slice of data. Only give them the bits they actually understand. They can clean that and stay away from this nightmare of a master sheet."

She blinks. The thought hits harder than expected. "Smaller files, one per department, then merge them later?"

Steve smiles. "Avoid BS doing any damage."

Alex looks down at her notes. He's right. Change the rule. Make the cleansing happen before creating the master load file, not inside it.

She grabs an orange sticky and presses the pen hard to the paper:

- **Extract ≠ Load.**
- **Departments own local files for cleansing.**
- **Greg merges cleansed files into the load file.**
- **Morgan loads the final version.**

The words look simple, but they hum with new logic.

They both stare at the list on the table. The ink still glistens while these four new orange notes glow under the lamp like a tiny declaration of victory. For a moment, it feels perfect, but then, almost in sync, they frown.

Steve speaks first. "You see it too?"

"The gaping hole in the middle?" Alex says.

"Exactly," he replies. "You've built two islands, but no bridge between them."

She laughs. "Story of my life. Extraction on one side, load on the other, and a Grand Canyon in between."

Steve picks up the wooden spoon again and gestures like a conductor. "So what do we call this bridge, then?"

"Transformation," Alex says, half-grinning.

They both burst out laughing, the word landing somewhere between revelation and punchline.

"Perfect," Steve says. "Now you just need to build it."

Alex leans over the table. "If the extracts and the load file are different, something has to reshape the data in between. That's where Sam and Jesse come in, but they can't work inside the extracts, and Greg's the only one allowed to touch the load file."

"So they need a bridge they can work on," Steve says. "A middle ground."

"A buffer," she says. "Not another spreadsheet. But a temporary space where the data can land, be cleaned and reshaped, then sent safely across."

Steve nods. "A bridge with guardrails."

The room stills. They both look down at the sprawl of colour across the table. Notes in yellow, pink, and blue layer the oak like a paper battlefield. The steam from the cassoulet drifts between them, twisting in the lamplight like a thought made visible.

Alex's eyes settle on a few familiar lines:

- *Vanessa: Compliance mask hiding chaos underneath.*
- *Sam: Enforce clarity and precision in documentation - no assumptions.*
- *Jesse: Document formal cleansing rules; make them visible.*
- *Jesse: Build the business case for a proper ETL tool.*
- *Morgan: Fix issues before the load, not after.*

It hits her. "What if Sam and Jesse don't have to keep fixing data by hand," she says slowly. "What if they define the rules and let a system apply them? The transformations run themselves."

Steve leans closer, squinting at the notes. "So instead of hunting through cells, they teach a system how to think. Tame the beast using protocol."

Alex smiles, the idea expanding as she speaks. "They stop cleaning. They start designing laws and apply them."

"Robo cleaners," Steve says, grinning.

She laughs. "Exactly. The buffer becomes their workspace. Their rules clean the data automatically before Greg ever touches it."

She picks up her pen again and writes a new line on an orange sticky:

- **Add buffer tables for transformation - Inside SAP?**
- **Transform of values inside the buffer.**
- **Automate transformation using rules.**

Steve reads over her shoulder. "Greg manages the structure, Sam and Jesse make the laws, Morgan loads the truth."

Alex leans back and studies the table. The fragments finally fit.

What once looked like chaos now reads like a process. People in the right places, logic doing the heavy lifting, and no one cleaning the same mess twice.

Then Steve asks the inevitable question that breaks the calm. "We've brainstormed ourselves into the perfect solution. But…"

Alex exhales, deflated. "Is this really possible?"

Alex stares at the notes, the ink now dry, the logic solid on paper but fragile in her chest. The kitchen hums with quiet. The fridge, the rain, the steady rhythm of Steve's breathing. For the first time in days, she can see a future that makes sense. Yet the thought creeps in before she can stop it.

"So," she says, "what do I even do with this?"

Steve looks up from the stove. "What do you mean?"

"I can't walk into a meeting and pitch a system based on wishful thinking. It's a theory, not proof."

He tilts his head. "Then get a second opinion."

"From who?" She gives a short laugh. "Everyone inside the company is either too busy protecting their patch or too scared to challenge the process. I agree, it looks good on paper. But it feels fragile. And showing this to anyone in my team feels dangerous."

Steve leans against the counter, arms folded. "So don't ask them. Ask someone who isn't directly involved. Fresh eyes. Fresh brain."

She nods slowly, mind already scanning through names. People she trusts are a short list. People she trusts and who know SAP even shorter. Then it hits her.

Eugene.

The quiet expert who'd once walked her through a migration fiasco in another project. The man who'd never panicked, never postured, and somehow made code sound like common sense. He'd told her once, *Every system has truth buried somewhere. You just need to ask the right question."*

She smiles. "Eugene. He'll tell me if this floats or sinks."

Alex takes her phone from her pocket and snaps a few photos

of the table, the colours glowing like tiny flags of reason. She removes the evidence. The battlefield becomes a dinner table again.

Steve sets down two plates and hands her a glass of wine.

"After dinner, one email," he says. "Then you're off duty."

She smiles. "Deal."

They eat, trading silence for comfort, and for the first time in days, the silence doesn't feel like pressure. Later, they curl up on the sofa, a blanket between them, the television already muttering through the opening scene of a terrible film. Steve squeezes her hand.

"You'll see," he says. "Tomorrow, proof."

Alex nods, half smiling. The project no longer feels haunted. She sees a glimmer of hope.

Captain's Log: Bridge Over Raided Data

R – Risks / Root Causes

- Data cleansing still depends on manual edits inside Excel "master" files.
- Departments overwrite each other's work.
- No controlled transformation layer between extract and load.
- *Migrate Your Data* templates are fixed, limiting flexibility to adapt cleansing logic.
- Errors multiply in the gap between extraction and loading.
- Without automation, rules exist only on paper, not in the system.
- Governance model untested - ownership defined but not yet enforceable.

A – Actions

- Introduce a **buffer layer** inside SAP to act as the *transformation zone*.
- Store departmental extracts separately in simple local files.
- Each department cleans its local files before submission.
- Automate cleansing through **rule-based transformations**.
- No changes after creating *Migrate Your Data* load file - one version, one truth.

I – Impacts

- Errors reduced before load rather than corrected after - less corrections.
- Clear ownership boundaries remove "too many hands" syndrome.
- Repeatable cleansing logic accelerates future migrations.

- Early success can justify investment in a formal ETL tool later.
- Morale boost: team finally working by design, not by accident.

D – Decisions / Dependencies

- Eugene to confirm that the buffer-table approach is viable.
- Claire to approve the ownership structure across departments.
- Richard to endorse the controlled-access model for all load files.
- Start with only one data object for proof of concept (suggested: Product Master).

Current state: **Brain dump complete. Recalibrating.**

10. SECOND PAIR OF EYES

Sunlight pours through the same blinds that once turned her desk into a cage. The *SAP Activate* certificate still hangs on the wall, now a witness rather than an accusation. The air smells of disinfectant and new beginnings, cool against her skin. A faint ring of old coffee circles the mousepad. The binders stay crooked but dependable. Even the half-empty bottle of water glints like proof of life. Nothing in the room has changed, only how she stands inside it.

She opens JIRA out of habit. The dashboard greets her with unlikely order. Where blank fields once mocked her, tidy summaries now appear, categories chosen, screenshots attached. She studies them, waiting for the illusion to crack. Then she spots Vanessa's name on half the updates and smiles. Of course. The calm assassin of chaos has visited. Order, it seems, spreads faster than panic.

She closes JIRA with a rare sense of relief and opens her inbox with careful optimism. One new message waits near the top, from Morgan: **Subject – Change Log Stats (Brace Yourself)**. Alex hesitates for a second, then clicks.

Weekend totals.

- *12,400 field changes in the last test cycle.*
- *3,200 reversed within twenty-four hours.*
- *4 users editing the same field on one product, cancelling each other out.*

- *173 base units corrected seconds before live transactions froze them.*
- *28 products flagged for deletion because their base unit is now untouchable.*

She scrolls further. The graphs look like heart monitors in distress, all spikes and flatlines. Morgan's closing note reads: *System behaving like a soap bubble. Looks shiny, pops easily.*

Alex exhales, leaning back. Proof, she thinks. If chaos had a metric, this would be it. The numbers hurt more because they confirm everything Sam, Jesse and Greg also warned her about. She closes the window and refreshes her inbox again, though she knows what she is really waiting for.

A new email slides into view. **Subject: Sanity Check – Brilliant and Terrifying.** Relief lands in her chest before she can help it. She opens the message.

Morning, Alex. Read your notes twice, once as a consultant, once as a human being. Both found something to admire and fear. Call me.

Alex wastes no second.

"Morning," says Eugene's voice, calm and unhurried. "Caught you before your second coffee?"

"Just about," she says, smiling. "You read my plan."

"I did. It is ambitious, possibly reckless, and I like it already. Tell me what you are trying to prove."

Alex takes a moment to compose herself.

"I need to show that this approach works before the board shuts it down. It needs to be fast, cheap, and good enough to survive a week of testing. That is the brief."

"Classic," he says. "And you are not wrong. Let us start with your wildest wild card."

"What about… Automate the data cleansing using predefined rules?"

"Yes. The tool already hides inside your SAP licence, in plain sight. Few know it's there. Define your business rules once, link them to the data buffer, and let them shout when something breaks. It's the quiet engine that keeps data clean."

A brief silence fills the room.

"What's it called? Alex asks.

"*Business Rule Framework*. BRF+. Engrave it in your memory."

Eugene senses from afar that Alex needs a moment to write it down.

"I built something similar two years ago," he continues. "Same chaos, smaller budget. It worked better than anyone expected."

Alex looks up, startled. "You've done this before?" The words sound more like relief than surprise. Then she refocuses on her notes. "Good. Because I just received some statistics, and they are ugly. More than a hundred base unit fixes, twenty-eight in permanent purgatory."

Eugene hums, the sound of a man weighing logic like currency. "Exactly. Business rules can catch these errors before they reach the load. They do not stop people from being careless, but they make carelessness visible, and hit the brakes."

Alex takes a moment to let his words land.

"The ETL idea," she says. "If we cannot buy one, can we build something ourselves?"

"Drastic," he says, amused. "But the kind of drastic that works. You already have the structure: extract the files, transform them through business rules, then load what survives. Call it an *ETL Light* prototype, and do it inside SAP."

"Why inside SAP?" Alex wonders out loud.

Eugene continues, warming to the topic. "Because the *Business Rule Framework* lives there. BRF+ can check incoming data against existing configuration and master data. It catches duplicates and code mismatches you'd never see in that giant master load file built with data extracts from your old systems."

Alex nods slowly. "So BRF+ is the backbone of our prototype."

"Exactly," Eugene confirms, a hint of amusement in his voice.

Alex hears him taking a sip, senses more revelations coming her way.

"And before you curse *Migrate Your Data* again, remember that it's a huge step up from the old LSMW days. This new Fiori app guides you through every load step. Definitely the right method for loading your data when no ETL tool is available. *Migrate Your Data* is not your villain. You focus on its strengths, not the weaknesses."

Eugene takes another sip to clear his throat.

"Those department-specific data extracts you mentioned," he says, "are ideal to feed your *buffer zone*. They're usually called *staging tables* or a *repository*, but stick with 'buffer' in your presentation. Leave the jargon alone."

Alex sniggers.

"Each team uses its own template with the fields they actually care about. They polish what they can and push it into this buffer. The business rules run the checks while you have lunch, and once everything passes, you export the clean data into the format the *Migrate Your Data* app expects."

"Sounds too good to be true," Alex says, cautiously optimistic.

"Exactly. Which leaves ownership," he says, dampening the euphoria slightly.

Alex leans back and takes a deep breath. "Yes. Four people edited the same field on the same product last week. Like the Chuckle Brothers: to me, to you, to me. Each department needs its own sheet, and one custodian should combine everything into the official template. Smaller sheets, fewer fingerprints."

Eugene says. "Sounds good to me. Proof is in the pudding, as they say."

"Pilot first?" Alex asks, a trace of trepidation in her voice.

"Always. Choose one data object, like product master. Define a manageable set, and run the loop end-to-end. Once it works, scale later."

Eugene adds, "And for clarity, that buffer can live inside the production system, but it must be ring-fenced and locked down for migration use only."

Alex nods. "A quarantine zone for data."

"Exactly," he says. "Temporary, controlled, and gone once the load is done."

"Control, Alt, Delete," Alex says with a smile on her face.

He leans back slightly. "Now for the cherry on top of your proposal. Export the data from that buffer so it drops cleanly into the exact format the *Migrate Your Data* app requires, column for column, sheet for sheet. No reshuffling, no missing headers."

Alex smiles. "The buffer output is the final, ready-to-load version? No edits, no patchwork?"

"Exactly," Eugene says. "Make it fit like a glove. The buffer does the hard work, and Greg can trust the data is ready to go."

She nods. "That saves Greg an enormous amount of time."

"Right," he says. "He might even buy you flowers."

"Good," Alex says confidently. "Keep it simple. Show the concept works. Make them believe it can be done."

For a moment the line goes quiet except for his steady breathing and the faint hum of the office air. She glances at the window. The light across the desk looks different now, the same pattern that once trapped her now shaped like order.

"Thanks, Eugene," she says.

"Any time. And Alex, when you show this to the board, do not apologise for being right."

The call ends with a soft click. The silence that follows feels earned.

Alex looks around the room. The same walls, the same certificate, the same desk, but the air has shifted. The blinds are open, the light clear. The office that once felt like a cell now feels like structure.

She closes her laptop, straightens a stack of papers, and breathes in the quiet hum that used to irritate her. Tomorrow she will walk back into the boardroom that nearly broke her. This time she will bring proof instead of promises.

A soft knock breaks her focus.

Vanessa steps in, two mugs in hand. The morning light catches her curls, turning them to copper at the edges, and the calm in her hazel eyes steadies the room. "You look like someone who has just solved world peace."

Alex smiles. "Closer to data peace. I think I've figured out how we stop the same mistakes repeating."

Vanessa hands her a mug, bracelets chiming softly as she moves. "How?"

"By finding the rules we already follow without realising. The checks we make after things go sideways, like wrong or missing codes, or values that trigger mayhem. If we can spot those patterns, we can automate to eliminate them before they reach the system."

Vanessa nods, practical as ever. "So you want the team to go through recent JIRA posts and look for these rules?"

"Brilliant suggestion. Anything that gets corrected more than once is probably a rule in disguise. Ask them to list every example. And I will forward an email from Morgan that also contains some clues for rules."

Vanessa's mouth curves into a quick, approving smile. "Turning chaos into clarity. I can brief that today."

Alex grins. "Perfect. Let's see what the system's been trying to tell us."

Vanessa heads for the door, setting one mug of coffee on the desk. Small faith in ceramic form. The room holds its breath. Clarity rests beside her now, warm and real.

Things are set into motion.

Now she needs to sell it.

Captain's Log: When There Is A Will, There Is A Raid

R – Risks / Root Causes

- Weekend change-log numbers confirm chaos is measurable, not hypothetical.
- 4 users editing the same field like it's a group hobby.
- Base-unit fixes and reversals still piling faster than approvals.
- No pre-validation step between Excel creativity and system disaster.
- Governance exists in theory, not in templates.
- Rigid *Migrate Your Data* structure still dictates the final load format.

A – Actions

- Prototype a lightweight ETL loop: extract, transform, load.
- Use BRF+ to define and link cleansing logic to buffer data.
- Create a quarantined buffer zone, ring-fenced and temporary.
- Buffer zone output must match the *Migrate Your Data* template.
- One custodian per departmental sheet, one final sign-off for the master load.
- Build pilot on Product Master only; prove, don't promise.
- Turn every repeated correction into a permanent rule.

I – Impacts

- Proof replaces panic; chaos now has metrics.
- Business rules expose carelessness before it spreads.
- Manual firefighting replaced by measured prevention.
- Greg's rework disappears - copy, paste, done.
- Morale improves when evidence beats theatre.

D – Decisions / Dependencies

- Eugene validates prototype design – external sanity secured.
- Vanessa leading rule-harvest from JIRA incidents.
- Greg responsible for final load file built directly from buffer zone output
- Board presentation pending: results first, approval second.
- Next dependency: a one-object pilot ready before governance meeting.

Current state: **Faith restored.**

11. RED LIGHT, GREEN LIGHT

The boardroom waits like a stage that remembers every failure. Glass walls, chrome fittings, the smell of polish and static. Every seat at the long table is filled, no refuge left for late arrivals or hesitation. The surface stretches the length of the room, spotless and cold, reflecting the lights above like an operating theatre. Alex feels the weight of it before she even crosses the threshold.

Richard stands at the head of the table, silver cufflinks catching the light. "Before we begin," he says, voice measured, "I want to introduce two guests joining us today. Linda, our CFO, and Derek, our CIO."

The names alone shift the atmosphere. Linda sits nearest the window, posture upright, every movement neat and deliberate. Her ash-blonde bob frames a face made for scrutiny. A fountain pen rests perfectly aligned beside a leather-bound notebook. Derek leans back a little in his chair, warm brown skin, trimmed beard, expression calm but calculating. His presence radiates quiet authority, the kind that reads code, budgets, and people with equal precision.

Alex swallows. Two additional heavyweights. Finance and technology. Numbers and systems. She feels like she has walked into a televised pitch, the kind where entrepreneurs are devoured politely before the cameras cut. For a brief, absurd second, she thinks, this is Dragon's Den. The thought makes her mouth dry.

Richard's gaze finds her. "You have the floor, Alex. We are short on time, so make it count."

The words hit like a sledgehammer.

She connects her laptop. The projector flickers to life, casting pale light across her face. Her reflection glimmers faintly on the glass wall, small and tense against the skyline. The hum of the machine fills the silence.

"Thank you," she says, voice even though her pulse isn't. "This last week has been an investigation. We looked at why testing keeps breaking down, why fixes never last, and why we repeat the same work again and again. Every discussion led to the same finding. The system does what we tell it to do, but not what we mean it to do."

She clicks to the first slide. Charts bloom across the wall in red and amber. "Here are the failures. Errors that should have been caught early. Data looks clean, loaded while dirty, and locked before correction. Every one of these issues cost time, money, and energy we no longer have."

She turns to face them. "This is not a technical problem. It is structural. We are relying on luck and goodwill instead of checks and rules."

Silence stretches. Linda's pen hovers, ready. Derek's eyes stay on the screen, unreadable. Richard folds his hands. Claire sits still, expression neutral.

Alex clicks again. A new slide appears: *The Ideal Scenario.*

"There is a perfect solution," she says. "A commercial ETL tool. It extracts, cleans, transforms, and loads data efficiently. It is built for this problem. It prevents human error entirely."

Nobody reacts, but she can feel the temperature drop. Linda's look could freeze reason itself.

Alex exhales quietly. "But we cannot buy it. Not now. The budget is closed. Procurement would take months. We are too late. So if we cannot buy the right tool, we must accept the consequence. We are asking people to succeed with tools that keep breaking their stride."

She lets the silence hang. The sentence feels dangerous, but it is true.

Richard's eyebrow lifts. "Go on," he says.

"Every night someone is still online after midnight fixing the same issue in a corrupted spreadsheet," she says. "We call it ownership, but it is erosion. The same people are absorbing the cost of poor process, and that cost is becoming personal. If we continue like this, commitment will turn into fatigue, and quality will follow it down."

Linda's pen clicks once. The sound cuts through the quiet like a verdict. "So you are asking us to purchase something we cannot afford?"

"No," Alex replies. "I am asking you to see what happens if we do nothing."

Linda leans back. "We have already invested millions in this project. What you are describing sounds like another cost centre disguised as innovation. Where are the numbers? What exactly do you save?"

Alex steadies herself. "In my experience, every delay *often* costs two days of retesting and easily compounds into hundreds of man-hours. A failed load sets off a chain reaction through several departments. Each fix is double-paid: once in overtime, again in draining motivation. We are wasting money quietly instead of investing it wisely."

Linda's eyes narrow. "Those are guesstimates, not facts."

"True," Alex says, "but that's because we don't measure what matters. Until we do, guesses are the only facts we have."

For a heartbeat, nobody moves. In a project full of dashboards, it's the first time silence produces a real metric.

Derek clears his throat. His voice is calm, deliberate. "Couldn't AI do this? Detect patterns, automate checks, maybe even predict issues before they happen?"

Alex meets his gaze. "AI can predict patterns, but it cannot correct what people have not cleaned. It multiplies logic. If our logic is wrong, it multiplies our mistakes."

She pauses, then smiles faintly. "Let me give you an example. I once asked an AI tool to write a short bio for my running club. Something light, a meet-and-greet piece. It came back impressive. Very polished, friendly, almost perfect. It even mentioned my two children, Joe and Sarah."

She glances around the table.

"I do not have children."

A few smiles surface, quick and uncertain, like a reflex.

Alex continues. "I asked the AI why it made them up. It said it added them for balance, because most women my age seem to have kids. Imagine if I had not checked the output. Imagine people reading that and believing it. A harmless bio becomes fiction, credibility disappears, and suddenly I need to pick up kids at school this afternoon."

Soft laughter ripples, then fades.

Her tone hardens. "Now imagine our company doing the same. Letting AI generate data, plans, or reports. And nobody is double checking because it sounds so confident. The damage would be instant and invisible. I am not against AI, but the dangers need to be understood before we trust it, and right now we do not have that understanding or the time to gain it."

Derek leans forward. "At least you proofread. Maybe that's the lesson."

Alex nods. "Exactly. We must check every AI output, but the time we think we're saving is the time we lose checking."

He exhales, rubbing a thumb across his temple as if conceding to a mild headache of logic. His mouth quirks. "Fair point."

She lets the silence settle, allowing herself a quiet breath of victory, then clicks to the next slide. *The Realistic Scenario.*

"If the perfect tool is off the table, we build one ourselves. A lightweight version using what we already own. It uses the standard business-rules engine included in our SAP licence. It checks every record before the load, flags issues, and stops bad data before it reaches the system. It is not expensive. It is not beautiful. But it works."

Linda stops writing. Her pen hovers above the page. Then, slowly, she looks up, one eyebrow lifting with the precision of a cost report.

Alex meets her eye. "Yes," she says. "Included. No extra licences. No hidden line item."

Linda tilts her head, half-smiling. The gesture says it all: a CFO's version of disbelief and delight.

Richard leans forward. "How long would that take?"

"One month for a pilot," she says. "The design is ready. The team has already started tracing repeat incidents in JIRA to find patterns that reveal hidden rules. Those patterns will feed the first validation set. We can prove the concept within the existing acceptance-testing window."

Linda raises her pen again. "And what is the risk if it fails?"

"Minimal," Alex says. "If it fails, we revert. We lose four weeks. If it succeeds, we stop bleeding hours permanently. The only real risk is standing still."

Derek crosses his arms. "Who owns it?"

"Each department owns its own sheet," Alex replies. "One custodian merges them into the main file. The rules check everything automatically. No version chaos, no hidden errors, no middle-of-the-night surprises."

"Governance through simplicity," Claire says suddenly.

Alex turns, startled. Claire's voice carries confidence, not sarcasm.

Claire leans forward, hands folded neatly. "It is smart," she continues. "People will resist at first, but they will adapt. They are tired of firefighting. This gives them boundaries, not bureaucracy."

Alex blinks. For a second she forgets to speak. Claire, of all people, agreeing?

Richard notices the hesitation. "You have her attention," he says. "Carry on."

Alex exhales slowly. "It is governance through ownership," she says, recovering her rhythm. "The system enforces structure so people can focus on work that matters. It protects people from process. That is how we keep them standing through go-live."

Linda interjects again. "If this is so simple, why did no one do it earlier?"

"Because simplicity hides in plain sight," Alex answers. "Everyone was too busy repairing what was broken to imagine prevention."

She pauses, the quiet stretching until even the projector seems to hold its breath. Then she adds, with a small shrug, "It took me a Sunday afternoon and a few glasses of wine to see the light."

The room bursts into laughter. Real, unguarded, the kind that shakes off formality. Even Richard leans back, smiling for once.

Alex laughs with them, tension leaving her shoulders in a wave she hadn't realised she was holding. For the first time, the boardroom feels almost human again.

Richard, now relaxed for the very first time, straightens slightly. "If we agree," he says, voice steady but softer, "what is your next step?"

"We pilot the framework on products Morgan identifies as notorious repeat offenders," Alex says. "We prove that validation before load prevents rework after. One month. One object. If it holds, we scale it."

"And if it doesn't?" Linda asks.

"Then I was wrong," Alex says, meeting her gaze. "But at least we will know why. We cannot say that about our current approach."

Linda studies her, then nods once, a gesture that feels more respectful than dismissive.

Richard shifts slightly, eyes still fixed on Alex. "You verified this?"

"Eugene Tan reviewed it," Alex says. "Independent validation. I knew him before I joined our company. He built a similar framework for another migration two years ago. He confirmed the logic and the design, and he is available if we want help running the pilot."

Richard leans forward a fraction. "He has done this before?"

"Yes," Alex replies. "Same problem, same budget limits. They cut their testing time in half."

Richard glances briefly at Claire, then at Linda and Derek. The decision lands between words. "Then we bring him in. If he knows how to steer this, let him lead the pilot. I want his report before we scale."

"Understood," Alex says, trying not to sound too stunned. For the first time that morning, she sees genuine movement in Richard's expression, the faintest nod of resolve.

He leans back, fingertips pressed together. "Good," he says quietly. "You verified before you sold, and now you deliver with evidence."

The words hang in the air. Approval, conditional but powerful.

Claire sits back, a small smile breaking through the professional mask. Derek looks thoughtful, already mapping out technical dependencies. Linda closes her notebook with a soft snap, the gesture crisp but not hostile.

Richard clears his throat. "All right," he says. "Run your pilot. Eugene joins as technical lead. If it holds, we formalise the framework."

Chairs scrape. The meeting dissolves into quiet movement. Papers shuffle. Voices murmur. The hum of the projector fades to a sigh.

Alex stays seated. Her hands rest on the same table that once hosted her humiliation. The surface still feels cool, but it no longer chills. She looks down at her faint reflection in the glass. For the first time, it looks like someone she can recognise.

Through the window, the city glints in sharp daylight. Claire and Derek stand near the door, talking in low tones. Linda leaves without looking back, but her expression is thoughtful, not cold. Richard closes his folder and looks up briefly. His nod is small but real.

Alex exhales. The boardroom hums quietly around her. It no longer feels like a courtroom or a den of dragons, but a place where something finally changed.

The red light had turned green. Thunderbirds Are Go!

Captain's Log: Raid Light, Green Light

R – Risks / Root Causes

- Executive scepticism about yet another "innovation" costing money.
- Fatigue is becoming more dangerous than actual data errors.
- Commercial ETL is off the table; internal build is the only way forward.
- Ownership confusion risks turning late-night fixes into a permanent culture.
- AI offers seductive shortcuts but multiplies flawed logic if left unchecked.
- "Estimates, not facts", could weaken conviction and fuel resistance.

A – Actions

- Present the case for the pilot, define scope, test, and validate.
- Eugene reviews the design and logic, ready to lead the pilot run.
- Trace repeated incidents through JIRA to harvest rules for the validation set.
- Assign ownership: departmental sheets, singular custodian, automated rules.
- Build a one-month pilot on repeat-offender products, prove value before scaling.
- Communicate risk honestly: doing nothing costs more than failing fast.

I – Impacts

- If successful, overtime and repeat errors dry up: fatigue relieved, money saved.
- Board and sponsors no longer firefight; they govern with evidence, not hope.

- Trust builds between teams; governance becomes simplicity, not bureaucracy.
- External expert's endorsement brings sudden legitimacy-and breathing room.
- One measured step forward: pilot may convert red light to green.

D – Decisions / Dependencies

- Board approve one-object pilot, pending Eugene's independent report.
- Derek to assess technical fit post-pilot for future scaling with limited budget.
- Claire supports governance model, predicts initial resistance then adaption.
- Next formal step: run pilot, present outcome, decide on full rollout or fallback.
- Scoreboard resets: this time, the cameras may catch success.

Current State: Some say it is not easy being green. I disagree.

12. WE CAN SEE CLEARLY NOW

Alex pushes through a curtain of damp leaves. The forest still glistens from last night's rain, each branch holding its own private secret of light. The air smells of pine and fresh rain. The mud beneath her boots is soft, yielding, a far cry from the frost that once cracked beneath her steps. Sunlight filters cleanly through the canopy, painting the path in long golden stripes. It is the same forest she walked through last winter, but everything feels different. Then, the world had been fog and fatigue. Today, it feels rinsed of both.

She came back on purpose. Not to escape, but to remember. The last time she was here she had been dragging the project, and herself, behind her like a heavy cart. Now she walks because she can. Each step lands sure, unhurried, her pace no longer dictated by deadlines or dread. The forest does not ask her to deliver anything. It simply receives her. The rhythm of her breath, her movement, the shifting light between trees, all of it feels like something she had been trying to build inside a system for months but only now understands.

The path bends and opens into the valley. The same view as before, but now stripped of fog and panic. The trees still stand in their exact order, disciplined without being commanded. The forest holds no meetings, tracks no deliverables, yet nothing here fails. It runs on balance, self-correcting and perfectly aligned. She smiles at the irony. All those governance slides, all those calls about alignment, when the answer was growing quietly under the sky.

Steve's voice reaches her from behind. "You walk faster when you're thinking."

She glances over her shoulder. He is half a step behind, as always. Calm, deliberate, sleeves rolled. His jumper smells faintly of coffee and clean air. He carries the same steady rhythm that once felt like resistance to her urgency but had, in truth, been the cure for it.

They reach the old wooden bench overlooking the shallow valley. It waits for them in the same place as before, weathered but unbroken, its surface polished smooth by rain and time. Last year she had sat here because her thoughts had collapsed before her legs did. Today she sits because stillness finally feels like strength. The wood is still scarred, but it feels warm against her palms. The mist that once hid the horizon has lifted. The valley stretches clear and wide, trees lined like rows of data finally reconciled.

Steve sits beside her, elbows on his knees. "You remember this spot?"

She laughs softly. "Hard to forget. Last time I couldn't breathe. Now the air finally belongs to me."

Silence folds around them, not heavy but earned. Birds move through the trees, flashes of small colour. A robin darts between branches, the same one perhaps, or its successor. The world continues its own project plan.

She draws a slow breath. "It has been a full year since that boardroom. Two rollout cycles later, and nobody calls it luck anymore."

Steve smiles. "Yes, the second rollout. Hard to forget. I actually saw you at the dinner table again."

She laughs. "Guilty as charged. We reused the same simple framework. No panic, no sleepless nights. Everyone owned their part. The pilot proved what culture can do before you spend a penny on technology. That gave Linda her evidence. She said, 'Now we know it is worth investing in the right tool.' Claire agreed immediately. She told Richard it was never about budgets, it was about behaviour."

Steve chuckles. "That sounds like her."

"She has mellowed. We all have." Alex looks across the valley. "They call it the governance model now. Same logic, fewer arguments. Derek is already running the vendor selection for the proper ETL solution. All offer the AI gadgets he desires. He calls it the brain that never sleeps."

Steve grins. "Kids and their toys."

Alex laughs. "Let him have it. As long as we humans stay in control."

They rise together and follow the path along the ridge. The ground gives slightly underfoot, damp but steady. The trees thin, letting light through in clean lines. Alex glances upward, the green glow reflected in her eyes. "A year ago, they called ETL overkill," she says. "Now it defines how we think."

Steve raises an eyebrow. "You built a prototype that changed the company."

She smiles. "We built it. Everyone did. I just started the map. Now it runs itself."

They walk until the trees open completely and the clearing spreads before them. Sunlight pours through the canopy, unfiltered and kind. It spills across the moss, catching on drops of rain, each one a tiny mirror flashing green. Alex stops, caught by the quiet precision of it.

"This view never changes," Steve says.

She shakes her head. "No, but we did."

He looks at her. "What changed most?"

She thinks for a moment. "We stopped chasing perfection and started building trust. The rest followed. Structure only matters when people believe in it."

They stand in the light, the forest breathing around them, calm and deliberate. The wind shifts through the branches like an old system running clean.

Alex closes her eyes for a moment, feeling the warmth on her face, the hum of the forest alive and steady. The world does not need her control anymore. It works because she let it.

When she opens her eyes again, the valley stretches in perfect alignment. The forest, the team, the project, all moving with the same quiet rhythm. No dashboards. No deadlines. Just balance.

She smiles, calm and certain. The system is whole again: the data, the people, the culture.

Clarity, at last, has found a home.

And this time, it will stay.

EPILOGUE

Well, look at us. Still standing.

If you've made it this far, congratulations again. You now qualify for hazard pay in emotional intelligence.

The project ended, technically speaking. Systems went live, egos rebooted, and someone somewhere still insists it was "smooth". Lies. But fine, we survived, and in project metrics that counts as victory.

Here's the part they never put in the 'lessons learned' deck: the system isn't the only thing that needed cleansing. People do. Me included. I came in believing SOAP was an interface thing. Turned out it was a mirror. Structured enough to start, open enough to listen, aligned enough to move, purified enough to let go. Sounds neat now. Felt like a breakdown at the time.

If you recognised yourself in any of it, don't panic. That means you're normal. Anyone who claims to love change management is lying or recently promoted. The rest of us are just trying to stop the madness before it fills another JIRA backlog.

Would I do it again? Of course. I'm a project manager. We forget pain faster than printers jam. But next time I'll bring stronger coffee and slightly lower expectations.

You're about to close the book, but before you do, a favour.

Use it. Quote it. Argue with it in meetings if you must. Let it save you from another corporate farce. If one line makes you laugh while the room burns, you're already halfway to clarity.

That's what SOAP gave me. Not perfection. Just peace with imperfection.

So, before you get back to your own project circus, do one thing for me: Document the truth while it's still fresh. Even if nobody reads it. Especially if nobody reads it. That's how the downward spiral ends and sanity begins.

Alright. That's my time.

You've got a world to fix, a system to migrate, and probably an inbox to regret.

Go on then. Off you go.

Make it Structured, keep it Open, stay Aligned, and when it all goes wrong, remember to Purify, preferably before the next status meeting.

And if it does explode again? At least you'll have a story worth telling.

Alex

AFTERWORD

Thank you for making it to the end.

You've just read a story about chaos, control, and the strange comfort of structure. The names were fiction, the patterns weren't.

SOAP isn't a slogan. It is a survival method: Structured. Open. Aligned. Purified.

Four words that turn messy projects into systems that work, and allow people to think clearly again.

Alex's story ends here.

Your journey continues at **sapsoap.com**, where SOAP brings clarity to real SAP migrations.

Isard

ACKNOWLEDGEMENT

This book was edited with AI support, steered at every turn by human hands, late nights, and too many post-its, and guided by my Universal AI Prompt.

universalAIprompt.com

ABOUT THE AUTHOR

Isard Haasakker

Isard has spent more than twenty-five years rescuing SAP projects from the edge of chaos.

Certified in S/4HANA and fluent in both functional and technical worlds, he translates complexity into systems that behave and people who sleep again.

From blueprints and test scripts to training packs and governance models, he builds clarity into every deliverable.
He mentors project teams on the Fast Implementation Track (F.I.T.) and writes books that turn failed projects into survival guides.

Find more frameworks, essays, and free resources at notiegeneration.com and sapsoap.com.

No tie. No ego. No excuses.

www.ingramcontent.com/pod-product-compliance
Lightning Source LLC
Chambersburg PA
CBHW060355180626
46817CB00008B/3025